ALL THE NONSENSE in my TEETH

MIKE HENSON
BARBARA BAKOS

happy yak

Tonight I brushed my teeth
and with the usual mess,
I found all kinds of nonsense
that you would never guess!

ALL THE NONSENSE
in my
TEETH

Quarto Knows

Quarto is the authority on a wide range of topics.

Quarto educates, entertains and enriches the lives of our readers—enthusiasts and lovers of hands-on living.

www.quartoknows.com

© 2022 Quarto Publishing plc
Written by Mike Henson. Text © 2022 Quarto Publishing plc
Illustrations © 2022 Barbara Bakos

Barbara Bakos has asserted her right to be identified as the illustrator of this work.

First published in 2022 by Happy Yak, an imprint of The Quarto Group.
The Old Brewery, 6 Blundell Street, London N7 9BH, United Kingdom.
T (0)20 7700 6700 F (0)20 7700 8066
www.quartoknows.com

A catalogue record for this book is available from the British Library.

ISBN: 978-0-7112-6628-5

Manufactured in Guangdong, China, TT122021
9 8 7 6 5 4 3 2 1

MIX
Paper from responsible sources
FSC® C016973

There were
breakfast hoops
and
ice-cream scoops...

An aeroplane
doing loop the loops!

An aeroplane? Now that's absurd!
Then to my shock, a flock of birds!

A marching group of stripy cats...

I can't remember eating that!

An **elephant** from Timbuktu
and hippos striding **two** by **two**.

And from my molars at the back,
a **panda,** painted white and black.

My canine teeth,
the ones up front,

hid a cyclist
doing a stunt!

When did I **let the nonsense in**
that came and **messed** up
my sparkling
grin?

In a day dream,
is that when
they all snuck in?
Hmm, was it then?

How they got there,
I don't know!
But I was sure
they'd have to GO!

And what was this that I now found,
making such a **dreadful sound**?
A big brass band that wouldn't hush!

I flicked them out,
with my brush.

Oh no! An ape called Geraldine
had started painting some teeth **green!**
But I prefer my smile to gleam,
so with some paste **I brushed them clean.**

Because I know I love to chew,
I need to keep my teeth like new.
I'd like to chomp on this and that
without this silly acrobat!

So...
back and forth, around and about,
I brushed and flushed the nonsense out!

And then, triumphantly, I said:
"Farewell to all...

... I'm off to bed!"

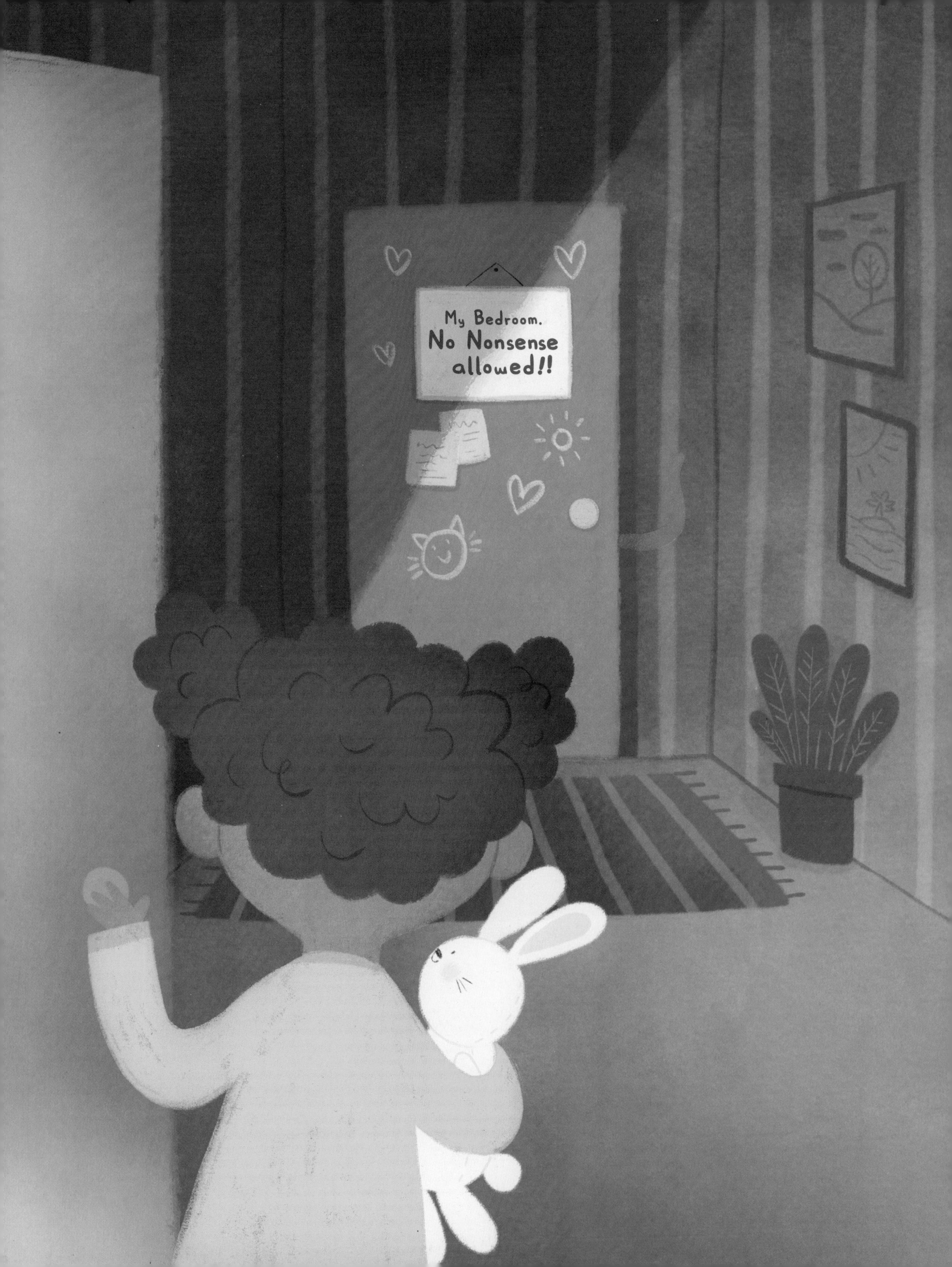
My Bedroom.
No Nonsense
allowed!!